The **Tray** of **Togetherness**

WRITTEN AND ILLUSTRATED BY
Flo Leung

Owlkids Books

Owlkids Books acknowledges the financial support of the Canada Council for the Arts, the Ontario Arts Council, the Government of Canada through the Canada Book Fund (CBF), and the Government of Ontario through the Ontario Creates Book Initiative for our publishing activities.

Published in Canada by Owlkids Books Inc.
1 Eglinton Avenue East, Toronto, ON, M4P 3A1

Published in the US by Owlkids Books Inc.
1700 Fourth Street, Berkeley, CA, 94710

Library of Congress Control Number: 2021951893

Library and Archives Canada Cataloguing in Publication

Title: Tray of togetherness / written and illustrated by Flo Leung.
Names: Leung, Flo, author, illustrator.
Identifiers: Canadiana 20210391030 | ISBN 9781771474627 (hardcover)
Classification: LCC GT4905 .L48 2022 | DDC j394.2614—dc23

Edited by Stacey Roderick | Designed by Alisa Baldwin

Manufactured in Shenzhen, Guangdong, China, in April 2022
by WKT Co. Ltd.
Job #21CB3375

MIX
Paper from responsible sources
FSC® C010256
www.fsc.org

A   B   C   D   E   F

ONTARIO ARTS COUNCIL
CONSEIL DES ARTS DE L'ONTARIO
an Ontario government agency
un organisme du gouvernement de l'Ontario

Canada Council   Conseil des Arts   Canada
for the Arts   du Canada

Publisher of Chirp, Chickadee and OWL
www.owlkidsbooks.com

Owlkids Books is a division of bayard canada

To Mom, Dusty, Ava,
and Po, for showing me
what togetherness is
all about

We're having a party—
a New Year party!

And I can hardly wait!

Grandma says we're celebrating
the new moon that begins
each brand-new year.

We're having a feast with everyone
—aunties and uncles, so many cousins,
and friends and neighbors, too.

We'll laugh and eat and stay up late.

We'll dance and sing and play music and games.

And we'll share the lucky sweets that fill our Tray of Togetherness.

Some for me,

and you,

and you!

We're having a party—a New Year party!

But first, an adventure to fill up our tray.

It has eight sections to fill. That's a lucky number and means our happiness will grow and grow.

Our lucky treats will help make our
New Year wishes come true.

It's like a game to find each kind
with its own special meaning.

Tangerines mean gold.
Look, we're rich!

Cashews for wealth.
And pistachios for happiness—
the more you eat,
the happier you'll be.

And there are
so many other delicious
New Year wishes ...

Candied coconut
for strong family ties

Watermelon seeds for a large family

Candied winter melon for good health

Candied kumquats

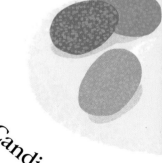

Peanuts for a long life

Candied lotus root
for abundance
year after year

for wealth

Candies for a sweet life

We choose each treat to make a wish.

We share each treat to pass on that wish.

From me,

to you,

and you!

This good luck comes in all sorts of colors—
red and gold and orange . . .
But I think the pink candies taste best.

I'll bring some for tomorrow's Show and Share.
And gold chocolate coins, too. Imagine,
a treasure you can eat!

These are some of the
sweet ways we share
our good wishes . . .

… and celebrate
togetherness as we begin
this brand-new year.

Our decorations
are up now, and our
tray is full of treats.

Some for me,

and you,

and you!

We're having a party—
a New Year party!

And now
everyone is
here!

Will you make a wish?

Will you *take* a wish?

Our Tray of Togetherness is filled with the many
sweet wishes we give each other . . .

...to celebrate this happy New Year!

About the Tray of Togetherness

The Lunar New Year is a festive time of year, full of celebration and happiness. It's also an important time to visit family and friends, and to begin the New Year with lucky traditions.

The Tray of Togetherness is one of those traditions. It is a special candy box that families fill with treats to offer guests. Each treat's name has a double meaning—the good wish it represents is often based on wordplay. For example, one way to say "tangerine" in Cantonese is *kam*, which sounds similar to the word for "gold." Offering guests tangerines means wishing them a full and wealthy New Year. And sharing candied lotus root is a way to wish your family and guests everything they need for a successful and plentiful New Year. That's because the Cantonese word for "lotus root" is *lin ngau* (pronounced "leen yow"), which also sounds like the phrase "having every year."

When I was much younger, the Tray of Togetherness was a family tradition that I looked forward to every year—mostly for the chance to eat as many candies as I could! And now that I'm a little older with a young family of my own, I feel grateful to have learned more about this delicious tradition, and to share these sweet New Year wishes with my growing family—and yours.